P9-CWE-409

9/0/0 Kenworthy #1196

TESSA KRAILING

The Petsitters Club

9. Pony Trouble

Illustrated by Jan Lewis

58070
J
KRA

First edition for the United States, Canada, and the Philippines published by Barron's Educational Series, Inc., 1999

Text Copyright © Tessa Krailing, 1999
Illustrations Copyright © Jan Lewis, 1999

All rights reserved.

First published in Great Britain in 1999 by Scholastic Children's Books, Commonwealth House, 1-19 New Oxford Street, London WC1A 1NU, UK
A division of Scholastic Ltd

No part of this book may be reproduced in any form, by photostat, microfilm, xerography, or any other means, or incorporated into any information retrieval system, electronic or mechanical, without the written permission of the copyright owner.

All inquiries should be addressed to:

Barron's Educational Series, Inc.
250 Wireless Boulevard
Hauppauge, New York 11788
http://www.barronseduc.com

ISBN 0-7641-0736-4
Library of Congress Catalog Card No. 99-20183

Library of Congress Cataloging-in-Publication Data
Krailing, Tessa, 1935–
    The Petsitters Club. 9. Pony Trouble / Tessa Krailing ; illustrated by Jan Lewis.
        p. cm.
    Summary: The Petsitters find themselves in trouble when Matthew, insisting that he knows horseback riding, agrees to exercise an independent-minded pony in his owner's absence.
    ISBN 0-7641-0736-4
    [1. Ponies—Fiction. 2. Horsemanship—Fiction. 3. Pets—Fiction. 4. Clubs—Fiction.] I. Lewis, Jan, ill. II. Title. III. Title: Petsitters Club, 9. IV. Title: Pony trouble
PZ7.K85855Pe   1999
[Fic]—dc21   99-20183
                                                                  CIP

Printed in the United States of America
9 8 7 6 5 4 3 2 1

Chapter 1

Yee-ha!

Monday morning—ugh!

Matthew hated Monday mornings. He found it hard enough to wake up any day of the week, but Mondays were the worst. He was still half-asleep when he walked through the school gates.

Then Hattie Groves bounced up to him.

"Hi, Matthew!" she said in her high, cheerful voice. "We went to the gymkhana on Saturday. And guess what —we won two ribbons!"

Matthew liked Hattie. She was a small girl with a freckly face and a wide, beaming smile. He just wished she wasn't quite so bouncy, especially first thing on a Monday morning.

She went on, "Of course, when I say *we* won them I mean me and Gazza. I've told you about Gazza, haven't I?"

Matthew stifled a yawn. "Lots of times."

"He's the bestest little pony in the whole world! Although he can be very tricky to ride. Can *you* ride, Matthew?"

"Yes, of course I can."

About two years ago, when he and his family stayed on a farm, the farmer had put him on a big horse and led him around the field. It felt fantastic! From that moment his dream had been to live in the Wild West and be a cowboy.

Hattie sighed. "I'm going to miss Gazza very much when I go to Australia. I know it's only for a month but it'll seem like ages." Her face brightened. "Matthew, can you *really* ride? You weren't just making it up?"

"Of course not," he said, annoyed.

Hattie beamed at him. "In that case, I've got a brilliant idea! While I'm in Australia, would you take Gazza out for a ride sometimes?"

Matthew finally woke up for the first time that morning. "You're asking me to ride your pony?"

Hattie nodded. "After all, you do belong to the Petsitters Club. And your ad says that you take care of any pet, large or small."

Matthew hesitated. "Yes, we do. But—"

"I keep him at the Springbank Riding Stables. That means he'll be well looked after while I'm away, but he does love going out for a really good gallop."

A really good gallop? Matthew liked the sound of that. He saw himself in a fringed jacket and a cowboy hat, riding tall in the saddle and yelling YEE-HA! as Gazza thundered over the hills.

"Yeah, okay," he said.

At that moment the bell rang for classes to start.

"Thanks, Matthew," said Hattie. "Talk to you later."

After school Matthew called a meeting of the Petsitters Club at Sam's house. Jovan said he couldn't stay long because his mother was expecting him home for dinner. Matthew's younger sister Katie said she couldn't stay long either because she had to feed Archie, her pet cockroach.

"This'll only take a minute," said Matthew. "I want to tell you about our new petsitting job."

When they arrived, Sam took them into the kitchen. "We'll have to keep our voices down," she warned. "My dad's working on a new comic strip."

Her father sat at one end of the kitchen table, surrounded by crumpled-up pieces of paper. He didn't even look up as they sat down quietly at the other end.

"Okay, Matthew," said Sam in a low voice. "What's this new job?"

Matthew told them about Hattie Groves and Gazza. The other three Petsitters listened in silence, their gazes fixed on his face. When he finished, nobody spoke for at least five seconds.

Then Sam said, "I didn't know you could ride, Matthew."

"He can't," said Katie.

"Yes, I can!" said Matthew fiercely. "We stayed on a farm once and the farmer let me ride his horse. You wouldn't remember because you were too little."

"I *do* remember," said Katie. "It was a big old carthorse and I rode it too. But that wasn't real riding. We didn't do trotting or cantering or galloping."

"*I* did," Matthew insisted. Although to be honest he wasn't sure now whether he did or not. But he *seemed* to remember galloping around the field. Or had that been in one of his cowboy dreams?

"I hate horses," said Jovan gloomily. "They have these big yellow teeth. One day my dad got called out to treat a horse with a bad leg, and when he bent down the horse nipped his bottom."

Katie laughed. Sam glanced nervously at her father, who seemed to have

stopped working and started listening.

"What else do we have to do?" Jovan asked Matthew. "Will we have to feed

Gazza and clean out his stable and stuff like that?"

"Pooh!" said Katie, holding her nose. "I'm not cleaning out any mucky old stables."

Sam's father made a curious snorting noise. They all turned to look at him but he pretended to be busy again.

"We won't have to do any mucking out," Matthew assured them. "I asked Hattie. She says the woman who runs the riding stables takes care of that. All we have to do is take him out for a ride sometimes."

"*You*, Matthew," said Jovan. "*You'll*

have to do the riding. It's no use asking any of *us* to do it."

Sam looked wistful. "I wish I could ride. I'd love to learn to ride more than anything in the world." She sighed, then added briskly, "Anyway, we can't let Matthew go alone. Remember our rule? Nobody goes petsitting on their own in case they get into trouble."

Jovan groaned. "Okay, but don't ask me to go near any horses!"

"Gazza isn't a horse, he's only a pony," Matthew said scornfully. "Anyone can ride a pony. I bet once I start riding I'll be really good at it. By the time Hattie comes back from Australia I bet I'll be galloping all over the place, rounding up cows and—and everything." He began to feel excited—so excited that he forgot about keeping his voice down and let out a blood curdling "YEE-HA!"

Sam's father put his head down on the table. His shoulders shook and he made an odd yelping noise, as if he was crying.

"Dad, are you all right?" Sam asked nervously.

"Fine." He sat up, wiping his eyes. "You've just given me an idea for my comic strip. I will call it 'Matt the Cowboy'."

The Petsitters looked at him doubtfully. They were never quite sure when Sam's father was joking.

"When does Hattie go to Australia?" Sam asked.

"In ten days, as soon as school is over," said Matthew. "But she wants us to meet her at the Springbank Riding Stables next Saturday morning."

Chapter 2

Gazza

"It's got to be easier than riding a bicycle," Matthew told Katie on the way to Sam's house. "I mean, a bike's only got two wheels. That's why, when you're learning to ride a bike, you keep losing your balance. But a pony has four legs, one at each corner, so it can't possibly fall over. It's just *got* to be easier."

17

Katie said nothing. She was in a bad mood. She wanted to go and play with her friend Alice, but Matthew insisted that she come with him and the others, otherwise she couldn't be a real member of the Petsitters Club.

"And I've been riding a bike since I was six years old," Matthew went on, speaking more to himself than to Katie.

"I can ride a bike with no hands, no feet, back-to-front, and upside-down. Riding a pony will be a piece of cake."

"No hands, no feet, no teeth," muttered Katie, which was what their father always said when Matthew boasted about his bike-riding skills.

"Yeah, well … you just watch me!" said Matthew.

At Sam's house, Sam and Jovan were already waiting for them. So was Sam's father, who had taken his rusty old car out of the garage to drive them up to the stables.

"Hi, Matthew," he said. "Got your riding gear?"

Matthew stared at him. "What riding gear?"

Sam's father grinned. "You know—boots, jodhpurs, hat. The sort of outfit people usually wear when they go riding."

Matthew went red. He didn't have any boots. Or jodhpurs. But he *did* have a hat! What's more, it was a real cowboy hat, given to him by his favorite uncle. He now wished he'd brought it with him.

Sam got into the passenger seat beside her father. "Oh, Dad! Matthew's not going to ride Gazza *today*. This is only a quick visit, otherwise I wouldn't ask you to take us. I know you've got a train to catch."

They arrived at the Springbank Riding Stables to find Hattie waiting for them in the yard. "Hi, Petsitters!" she called when they got out of the car. "Come and meet Gazza."

Beside Hattie stood a chestnut pony with short sturdy legs, rounded sides, and a thick black mane. He watched the Petsitters approach with a wary eye.

"Oh, isn't he beautiful!" Sam exclaimed.

"Can I stroke his nose?" asked Katie.

"Yes, but gently," said Hattie, keeping a tight hold on the rope attached to Gazza's red halter.

Katie stroked Gazza's nose very, very gently. Sam joined her, patting his shaggy neck. "You are lucky, Hattie," she said. "I'd love to have a pony."

"They're expensive to keep," said Hattie. "Especially if you have to pay for them to live at a stable, like I do. But I couldn't keep Gazza at home because we don't have a field."

Gazza tossed his head. He began to shift about restlessly on his short legs.

"He's getting nervous," said Hattie. "Come into the tack room, Matthew, and I'll show you where I keep his saddle and bridle. Sam, would you mind holding Gazza?"

"I'd love to." Flushed with pride, Sam took the rope. She turned to her father. "Dad, do you mind waiting a bit longer?"

He glanced at his watch. "No, I'm okay for another ten minutes. I'll get my pad from the car and make some sketches."

The other three Petsitters followed Hattie. She took them into the tack room where a tall, fair woman in jodhpurs was busy polishing a saddle.

"Hello, Mrs. Baker," said Hattie. She turned to the Petsitters. "Mrs. Baker runs Springbank Stables. She knows all about horses, so if you have any problems she's the person to talk to."

"Hello, Hattie." Mrs. Baker put the saddle down. "These must be the Petsitters you told me about. Who's the boy who's going to be exercising Gazza?"

"I am," Matthew said proudly.

Mrs. Baker looked at him with piercing blue eyes. "Experienced rider, are you?"

Before he could answer, Hattie said, "Matthew's an expert. All the Petsitters are. It says so in their ad."

Mrs. Baker seemed unconvinced. "Perhaps he should take Gazza out for a trial ride to see if they get along together."

"Good idea!" Hattie turned to Matthew. "Would you like to?"

"Ride Gazza *now*?" Matthew stared at her. "But I'm not wearing the proper clothes."

"Oh, don't worry about that!" said Hattie. "I often wear my jeans for riding. All you need is a hard hat."

"I've got a hat," said Matthew. "But it's at home."

"I'll lend you mine." She produced a helmet with a strap. "Here you are. Try it on."

Matthew shook his head. It wasn't nearly as cool as his cowboy stetson. "I don't think I'll bother," he said.

"Oh yes, you will!" said Mrs. Baker firmly. "Nobody goes riding without a hard hat. If you fall off you could do serious damage to yourself."

"Mrs. Baker's right, Matthew." Hattie jammed the helmet on top of his head and fastened the strap.

Matthew scowled. Whoever saw a cowboy wearing a stupid helmet? Next time he came he'd make sure to bring his stetson.

Hattie said, "Alright! Let's get Gazza saddled up."

Chapter 3

Hattie's Hat

Meanwhile, outside in the yard, Sam was talking quietly to Gazza.

"I wish I had a pony like you. If I did I'd ride you every single day and we'd gallop and gallop and gallop. Then I'd bring you home and take off your saddle and brush you until your coat shone. I wouldn't even mind cleaning out your stable, no matter how mucky it was. Because I think you're beautiful!"

Gazza made a little wickering noise. He pushed his nose against her pocket.

"Next time we come I'll bring you something to eat," she promised.

She glanced at her father, who was busy drawing in his sketchpad, and noticed he had a big grin on his face.

"What's so funny?" she asked.

"My new cartoon character," he said. "Matt the Cowboy. Hello! Here he comes!"

He pointed to the tack room. Matthew came out of the door, followed by Hattie, Jovan, and Katie.

Sam said, "I don't think he looks very happy."

Dad chuckled. He called out, "Hi, cowboy. I like your hat!"

Matthew scowled at him. "It's not mine, it's Hattie's."

"Why are you wearing Hattie's hat?" Sam asked.

Matthew squared his shoulders. "Just going for a trial ride," he said.

Sam sighed enviously. "You are lucky, Matthew!"

She paid close attention while Hattie showed them how to first put on the saddle and then the bridle. *One day I'll learn how to do this*, she thought. *And then I'll be able to ride a pony just like Gazza.*

Hattie turned to Matthew. "Ready to get on?"

He put one foot in the stirrup and grabbed the front of the saddle. But at that moment Gazza moved forward and Matthew was left hopping around on one leg.

"Stand still, Gazza," commanded Hattie. "Here, Matthew, I'll help you."

She grabbed Matthew's hopping leg and heaved him into the air. He landed plonk! on his stomach across Gazza's back.

Katie shouted with laughter. "You're supposed to *sit* on the saddle, not lie down on it," she said scornfully.

Somehow Matthew managed to struggle upright. By now Mrs. Baker had come out of the tack room to join the watching crowd. He grabbed the reins and shook them purposefully. "Okay, let's get movin'."

Hattie said, "You'd better wait until I've adjusted the stirrups. Your legs are longer than mine." She lengthened the leather straps and slipped Matthew's feet into the stirrups. "How's that?"

"Fine, just fine," he drawled. He squeezed Gazza's sides with his heels. "Git along, little pony. Yee-ha!"

Gazza looked surprised. He turned his head as if trying to see who was sitting on his back.

Dad put away his sketchpad. "Alright, Petsitters. Time to go."

Matthew looked disappointed. "Already?

I was looking forward to a good gallop."

"Sorry, but if we don't leave now I'll miss my train."

Reluctantly Matthew slid to the ground. He took off the helmet and handed it back to Hattie.

Mrs. Baker stepped forward. "Is

Matthew quite sure he wants to do this petsitting job? It's a big responsibility, riding somebody else's pony. I can easily find someone to exercise Gazza while you're away, Hattie."

Matthew said quickly, "No, I'll do it. I'm a little out of practice but it'll come back to me in no time." He turned to Hattie. "You go to Australia and have a wonderful time. We won't let you down. Will we, Petsitters?"

Jovan and Katie shook their heads. Sam breathed a sigh of relief. She couldn't wait to visit the stables again and learn as much about ponies and riding as she possibly could.

Chapter 4

Matt the Cowboy

Matthew was thoughtful on the drive back to Sam's house. He was sure that Mrs. Baker didn't believe him when he said he was an experienced rider. But he *could* ride, he knew he could! All he had to do was stay in the saddle and make Gazza turn left or right by pulling on the reins. Easy as riding a bike.

"You're very quiet, Matthew," said Sam's father, speaking over his shoulder. "Are you sure you want to do this job? You heard what Mrs. Baker said. She can easily find someone else to exercise Gazza."

"But he *does* want to do it," said Sam. "Don't you, Matthew?"

"Yeah, sure I do," he drawled, in his best Texan accent.

Jovan said, "I wouldn't ride Gazza if you paid me a thousand dollars!"

"*I* would," said Sam. "Dad, can I have riding lessons, please?"

Her father sighed. "Sorry, Sam, but learning to ride is an expensive business. We can't afford it. Unless, of course, my new comic strip is a huge success."

Sam giggled. "You should see Dad's new comic strip, Matthew. It's all about you riding Gazza."

Matthew didn't say a word. His head was already buzzing with pictures of himself galloping on Gazza ...

of Gazza jumping over a gate ...

of Gazza bucking like a Wild West bronco …

of himself lying on the ground with a broken leg …

No, that last picture was a mistake. He put it firmly out of his mind.

By the time Hattie left for Australia Matthew was feeling confident. He had found a book on cowboys in the library and reckoned he now knew all about bronco-busting and rodeos and rounding up cattle. When the time came for them to go to the stables he took his stetson hat down from the attic. Then he put on a checkered shirt, fastened a leather belt around the waist of his jeans, and looked at himself in the mirror.

Yeah, that was more like it! Wearing the proper clothes made all the difference.

"Katie!" he called. "Katie, you comin' to the stables?"

Katie appeared holding Archie, her pet cockroach. "Sorry, I can't," she said. "I'm going over to see my friend Alice. Anyway, I'm an expert on creepy-crawlies, not ponies."

"Okay," said Matthew with a shrug. He went off to get Jovan from his house.

Jovan appeared on the doorstep clutching a box of paper tissues. "Sorry, I cad cub," he said. "I godda bid of a code."

"Eh?" said Matthew.

Jovan blew his nose. "I can't come because I got a bit of a cold," he said, making an effort to speak more clearly.

"But you've gotta come!" said Matthew. "This is the biggest petsitting job we've ever had. The biggest animal, anyway. I'll need some help roundin' him up."

Jovan sighed. "You'll be sorry if I ged dubodia."

"Dubodia? Oh, I guess you mean pneumonia." Matthew frowned. He didn't want to be unkind, but he *did* want Jovan to come with him to Springbank

Stables. Anyway, apart from watery eyes and a red nose Jovan didn't look all that sick.

"You won't get pneumonia, Jo," he said firmly. "Fresh air is good for you. Better than stayin' in a stuffy house. C'mon."

"Oh, all ride." Reluctantly, Jovan grabbed a box of tissues and shut the door behind him.

When Sam saw them she called her father. "Dad, come and look at Matthew. And you'd better bring your sketchpad."

"Oh, my hat!" said Sam's dad, coming out of his den. "Or rather, *your* hat, Matthew. That stetson looks really cool. Mind if I make a quick sketch? Then I'll get the car out and run you kids up to the stables."

Sam said suspiciously, "You haven't got to catch a train or anything?"

"Oh, I won't stay. I'll leave you there and come back to pick you up in a couple of hours. Will that be long enough?"

Jovan sniffed. "Quide log enough. I'll have god dubodia by then for sure."

The first person they saw when they arrived at the stables was Mrs. Baker. "Hello, Petsitters," she said. She stared at Matthew's stetson. "I hope you're not intending to ride in *that*? It won't give you any protection if you fall off. You'd be far better off wearing Hattie's helmet."

"No, thanks," said Matthew firmly. "I'd rather wear my own."

"Anyway, he's not going to fall off," said Sam. "Are you, Matthew?"

"No, I sure ain't!" Matthew stuck both thumbs into his leather belt and stood with legs apart. He wished now he'd brought some gum to chew, like they did in Western movies.

"Hmmm," said Mrs. Baker. "Well, we'll argue about that after you've caught Gazza."

Sam looked around the yard. "Where is he?"

"In the field," said Mrs. Baker. "You'll have to take his halter—it's in the tack room—and bring him back here to saddle up. I warn you, he can be difficult to catch."

"Oh, that's all right," Sam patted her pocket. "I've brought some bits of carrot. We'll catch him easily. Come on, Petsitters."

Chapter 5

"Let's go, go, go!"

Armed with Gazza's halter, the Petsitters were off. But when they got there they discovered there were three ponies in the field—and from a distance they all looked alike.

"Which one's Gazza?" asked Matthew.

"Let's call his name and see which one comes," said Sam. She fished in her pocket. "Gazza! Gazza, come and see what I've got. Lovely, crunchy carrot, yum yum!"

All three ponies turned their heads. All three came trotting towards them.

"Now you can tell!" said Sam triumphantly. "He's the smallest one. Get ready, Matthew."

Matthew climbed onto the gate, holding the halter. But when Sam held out the carrot, all three ponies clustered around her. Matthew took aim at the one he hoped was Gazza, but the pony seemed to guess what he was doing and quickly stepped sideways. This left Matthew leaning over at a dangerous angle. He dropped the halter and clutched at the gate, trying to keep his balance, but it was no use. All of a sudden, he toppled over into the field, landing softly on the grass. Startled, all three ponies moved away.

Matthew scrambled to his feet. "What we need is a lasso," he said. "That's what cowboys use to catch the wild mustangs."

"But Gazza isn't a wild mustang," Sam pointed out. "He's a tame pony. I bet I could catch him."

She climbed over the gate and picked up the halter. Then, keeping it hidden behind her back, she looked straight at Gazza. Slowly and steadily she walked towards him, holding a piece of carrot on the palm of her free hand. Gazza stretched out his neck and gently took it between his lips. Sam patted his nose, while with the other hand she swiftly slipped the halter over his head and fastened it.

"Well dud, Sab!" said Jovan.

Matthew thought it was well done too, but he was a little annoyed that Sam was able to catch Gazza when he had failed. He said gruffly, "Okay, bring him over here. I'm gonna ride him back to the stables."

"Bud he hasn't got a saddle od," said Jovan.

"I'll ride him bareback like they do in rodeos."

Matthew perched on top of the gate. When Sam brought Gazza close enough he climbed onto the pony's back. Oops! It felt slippery without a saddle and there was nothing to grab hold of except Gazza's mane.

"Okay, let's get's movin'," he said. "Yee-ha!"

Sam glanced up at him uncertainly. "I'll have to lead him, Matthew. He's not wearing a bridle."

"That's okay," said Matthew impatiently. "Go, go, go!"

But instead of go-go-going Gazza lowered his head to munch at the grass.

Taken by surprise, Matthew toppled forward. Slowly, gently, gracefully, he slid down Gazza's neck to land kerplop! on the grass.

Sam looked down at him nervously. "Are you all right?"

"Yeah, fine." Matthew scrambled to his feet. His stetson had fallen off but luckily not his glasses. "Cowboys fall off all the time at rodeos."

"Bud nod when the horse is standing still," Jovan pointed out.

Ignoring him, Matthew picked up his stetson and climbed onto the gate again. "Okay, Sam," he said. "And this time don't let him eat the grass."

Meekly Gazza allowed himself to be led close to the gate. Matthew slid onto his back and said, "Alright, let's go. YEE-HA!"

Sam pulled on the rope. But as Gazza moved forward he gave a skittish little wiggle of his hindquarters. Matthew slipped sideways and, slowly, gently—but this time not so gracefully—landed kerplop! on the grass.

Jovan picked up Matthew's stetson and handed it back to him. "I think Mrs. Baker's ride," he sniffed. "If you're going to keep falling off, you'd be buch better off wearing Haddie's had."

Annoyed, Matthew jammed the stetson back on his head and adjusted his glasses. "I am NOT gonna keep fallin' off!"

He climbed onto the gate and once more commanded Sam to bring Gazza close. As soon as he was astride Gazza's back he said, "Alright, let's go. YEE-HA!"

But once again Gazza wiggled his hindquarters and Matthew—slowly, gently, and not at all gracefully—landed kerplop! on the grass.

Furious, he got to his feet. He adjusted his glasses and picked up his stetson.

Sam said, "You know, Matthew, I don't believe real cowboys do much bareback riding. They leave it to people in circuses. If you wait till Gazza's saddled up you'll be able to ride him easily."

Matthew hesitated. He hated giving up, but what Sam said made sense. Riding Gazza with a saddle and bridle would be much, much easier than trying to ride him bareback.

"Okay." He snatched the rope out of Sam's hands and set off on foot. "Open the gate and let's go, go, go!"

Chapter 6

"I Don't Believe He Can Ride."

Deep in thought, Sam followed Matthew, Jovan, and Gazza back to the stables. She was beginning to suspect that Matthew wasn't as good a rider as he claimed to be. In fact, she didn't think that he could ride at all! If she was right, this petsitting job could turn out to be a disaster.

She caught up with Jovan. "Jo," she

said quietly so that Matthew couldn't hear. "Jo, I don't believe he can ride."

"I dod believe he cad either," said Jo. "Whadda we going to do?"

"Maybe we could just take Gazza out for a walk. I know we promised Hattie we'd exercise him, but we didn't say how. If we took him for a walk that would be exercise, wouldn't it?"

Jovan looked doubtful. "But nod very *fast* exercise. If Gazza wanted to gallop dud of us could keep ub with hib."

"No, I suppose not. But—"

"What are you two guys mutterin' about?" Matthew asked over his shoulder.

"Nothing," said Sam quickly. "That is, we were wondering … do you think you *should* try to ride Gazza, Matthew?"

"Yeah, of course!" He sounded astonished that she should even ask. "I can't wait to take him out for a gallop."

He *sounded* confident enough, but Sam was worried. What if he took Gazza out for a "gallop" and fell off? He could be badly hurt and Gazza might run away—and Mrs. Baker would be furious.

And what on earth would Hattie say when she got back from Australia?

Back in the stable yard they found Katie waiting for them. Matthew stared at his sister in surprise. "I thought you were too busy to come. What made you change your mind?"

"Alice has a riding lesson, so I came with her," Katie replied.

Mrs. Baker appeared from the tack room, followed by a small figure in jodhpurs and riding boots. For a moment Sam hardly recognized Alice Hope, Katie's friend. Most of her head was hidden by a large helmet. Only her bangs showed and a pair of large brown eyes.

"Hello, Alice," said Sam. "I didn't know you could ride."

Alice nodded, solemn-faced. Sam had never heard her speak. Usually Katie had to speak for her because she was so shy.

"Alice is one of my best pupils," said Mrs. Baker. "Did you have any problems catching Gazza?"

"Nothin' we couldn't handle," said Matthew. "Sam, could you hold him while I fetch his gear from the tack room? Comin', Jo?"

He gave Sam the rope and marched across the yard, followed by Jovan.

Gazza nuzzled against her pocket, searching for more carrots. "*Please* don't make Matthew fall off again," she whispered. The pony pricked up his ears as if he was listening to her. "*Please* let him ride you so he doesn't look silly."

So that none of us looks silly, she added silently. The honor of the Petsitters Club was at stake! If they messed up this job, no one would ever ask them to look after their animals again. She glanced uneasily at Mrs. Baker, who was helping Alice tack up a small gray pony on the other side of the yard.

Matthew came out of the tack room carrying the saddle, followed by Jovan with the bridle. He flung the saddle over Gazza's back and fastened the girth. So far so good. But then he took the bridle from Jovan and stared at it helplessly, as if it were some kind of puzzle.

"Would you like me to try?" Sam offered. "I watched Hattie doing it the other day."

"Yeah, okay," said Matthew.

She slipped the metal bit into Gazza's mouth, just as Hattie had done, and fastened the straps. "There, now he's ready."

"Wait!" Mrs. Baker came towards them holding Hattie's helmet. "You can wear your stetson if you like, but you *must* wear this underneath it. I insist."

Before Matthew could protest, Mrs. Baker jammed the helmet onto his head and fastened the strap. Scowling, he put the stetson on top. It looked so odd that Sam wanted to laugh, but somehow she managed not to. She noticed that Alice was now sitting astride the gray pony, watching them.

Mrs. Baker said, "Pull down the stirrups and I'll give you a leg up."

This time Matthew managed to land fair and square in the middle of the saddle. Sam began to feel more hopeful. Perhaps it wasn't going to be a disaster after all.

Matthew put his feet into the stirrups and gathered up the reins. He looked pale but determined. "Okay, let's go," he said to Jovan, who was holding the bridle.

"Wait!" said Mrs. Baker again. She pulled up the saddle girth another couple of notches. "If you don't have it tight enough you'll slide off. And those stirrups need adjusting."

"Yeah, they should be much longer," said Matthew. "Like a cowboy's."

Mrs. Baker raised her eyebrows. Sam said quickly, "He does have quite long legs. Even Hattie said so."

Without another word Mrs. Baker made the stirrups longer. Matthew squeezed the pony's sides with his heels. Gazza moved forward, but with the same skittish little wiggle of his hindquarters that he'd done in the field. Once again Matthew slid sideways, but this time he managed to clutch at the saddle and pull himself upright.

"I wish he wouldn't *do* that!" he complained.

"Do what?" asked Sam.

"Wiggle his backside. He does it every time."

Mrs. Baker smiled. "All ponies have their funny little ways. When Gazza does that we say he's dancing. Don't worry, you'll soon get used to it."

Sam groaned inwardly. That was all they needed—a dancing pony!

By now she was seriously worried. Somehow she had to stop Matthew from making himself look foolish—*and* ruining the Petsitters' reputations!

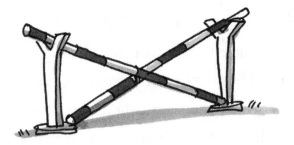

Chapter 7

School for Ponies

Matthew gathered up the reins again. "Okay, time to hit the trail," he drawled.

"Wait!" said Mrs. Baker for the third time. "May I ask where you plan to go?"

He shrugged vaguely. "I thought maybe we'd head for the open prairie."

Mrs. Baker raised her eyebrows. "The open prairie? That might not be popular with the local farmers. Besides you could easily get lost. Why don't you use our school?"

"School?" repeated Matthew, puzzled.

She nodded. "It's around the back of the stables. That's where Alice and I are going now. You can come along if you like."

Sam looked relieved. "That sounds like a good idea. Doesn't it, Matthew?"

"We-ell…" Matthew began uncertainly.

"I think it's a great idea," said Jovan. "Can we all come?"

"If you like." Mrs. Baker motioned to Alice and opened the gate.

Matthew urged Gazza forward. This time he was ready for the wiggle and managed to stay in place. As they followed Alice around the back of the stables he wondered what a school for ponies looked like. He imagined a large classroom full of ponies sitting at tables with their books open.

It turned out to be a small, oblong field enclosed by a wooden fence. When Jovan saw it he said, "It's a good thing the ground's covered in sand. That means it won't hurt too much if you fall off again."

"Oh, did you fall off?" asked Katie, staring at her brother.

Matthew didn't answer. He was too busy staring at what was *inside* the school.

JUMPS!

Okay, so they were fairly low and there were only two of them. But they were real jumps, with red-and-white poles, the kind you see at horse shows. For the first time, Matthew felt a pang of doubt. Did cowboys take their ponies over jumps? He couldn't remember.

Mrs. Baker glanced at his face. "If I were you I'd walk Gazza quietly around the outside until you get used to riding him," she suggested.

Matthew squeezed Gazza's sides with his heels. Out of the corner of his eye he could see Alice riding at the jumps. As she cantered towards the poles she called out "Hup!" and the little gray pony sailed over with room to spare. They made it look so easy.

Suddenly, he realized that Gazza was becoming restless, shifting sideways and making odd little movements like a rocking horse. "Better keep a tight hold of the reins," warned Mrs. Baker. "He wants to jump."

Too late. Gazza had already decided that anything the little gray pony could do, he could do better! With a rebellious toss of his head he set off for the nearest jump, with Matthew hanging desperately to the front of the saddle. And he might have *stayed* in the saddle, if only Gazza hadn't done one of his little wiggles on takeoff. As it was, Gazza cleared the jump easily—but Matthew didn't.

He flew into the air and landed heavily on his bottom.

The others rushed to help him up.

"What happened? Are you all right? Did you hurt yourself?"

He brushed himself off, too shaken to answer. The sandy floor of the school had felt much harder than the grassy field. And this time he hadn't fallen so gently.

Jovan picked up his stetson and handed it to him. "It's a good thing you were wearing Hattie's hat."

Alice dismounted from her pony and helped Mrs. Baker catch Gazza. They both came to join the group surrounding Matthew.

Mrs. Baker looked at him with some sympathy. "Do you want to continue? Or have you had enough for today?"

Matthew hesitated. The truth was he'd had more than enough. In fact, he'd changed his mind about being a cowboy. But he hated to admit it to the others.

Then Sam said, "I think Gazza's too small for you, Matthew. Your legs hang down so far it makes it difficult for you to ride him."

Jovan nodded. "You said yourself that you're more used to riding great big farm horses."

"Well ... yes, I am," Matthew agreed. "But I did promise Hattie—"

"I don't think Hattie realized how tall you are," Sam said quickly. "It's like asking you to wear the wrong size clothes. Gazza just doesn't fit you properly."

Still Matthew hesitated. He hated the idea of letting Hattie down. And what about the Petsitters' claim that they could look after any pets, large or small?

"*I* know!" said Katie. "Why don't we ask Alice to exercise Gazza? She's a really good rider."

"*And* she's the right size," said Jovan.

Matthew said reluctantly, "But she's not a Petsitter…"

"We could make her a sort of special helper." Sam turned to Alice. "What do you think? Would you like to be our pony expert?"

Alice went pink with pleasure. She nodded her head so vigorously that her helmet nearly fell over her bangs.

"Sounds like an excellent idea," said Mrs. Baker. She took the gray pony's reins from Alice and handed her Gazza's. "Why don't you give him a workout right now? He's obviously longing to go over the jumps."

Matthew breathed a secret sigh of relief. It was true, of course. Gazza was much too small for his long legs. That's why he hadn't been able to ride him. What a lucky thing Sam had figured out what the problem was!

"Everything go all right?" asked Sam's dad when he came to pick them up in the car.

"Yeah, it worked out okay in the end," said Matthew. And he explained exactly what had happened.

Sam's dad chuckled. "That's more or less how I imagined it. Except for Alice, of course. I must put her into my comic strip right away."

"And guess what, Dad!" Sam said excitedly. "Mrs. Baker said she'd been watching me with the horses and she was impressed by the way I handled them.

She asked if I'd like to help out at the stables sometimes, so of course I said yes. And then she said if I work hard she'll teach me to ride. Oh, I can't wait!"

Matthew felt a brief pang of envy. Mrs. Baker hadn't seemed at all impressed by the way *he* handled horses. But then he remembered how cleverly Sam had figured out why he couldn't ride Gazza, and decided she deserved some good luck.

Jovan said slowly, "The funny thing is, my cold seems to have gotten better. It must be the fresh air."

Matthew grinned. "So that means you won't be getting dubodia after all."

"Dubodia?" repeated Jovan, puzzled. "Oh, I suppose you mean pneumonia. What's the matter, Matthew? Are you getting my cold?"

"No, I feel fine," said Matthew. "Just fine."

And it was true, he did feel fine. Okay, so his dream of becoming a cowboy would have to be put on hold for a while. But one day, he felt sure, he'd find a horse big enough for his long legs and then YEE-HA! Matt the Cowboy would ride again!

The End